RICHIE F. DWEEBLY THUNDERS ON !

Malcolm Yorke
with illustrations by
Margaret Chamberlain

DORLING KINDERSLEY
LONDON · NEW YORK · STUTTGART

A DORLING KINDERSLEY BOOK

First American Edition, 1994
2 4 6 8 10 9 7 5 3 1
Published in the United States by
Dorling Kindersley, Inc., 232 Madison Avenue
New York, New York 10016

Library of Congress Cataloging-in-Publication Data

Yorke, Malcolm, 1938–
Richie F. Dweebly thunders on / written by Malcolm Yorke; illustrated by
Margaret Chamberlain. — 1st American ed.
p. cm. — (Teachers' secrets)
Summary: Mr. Dweebly's students do not suspect that their boring teacher is
secretly the fantabulous rock star Rab Thunder.
ISBN 1 56458-199-3
[1. Teachers—Fiction. 2. Schools—Fiction. 3. Rock music—Fiction.]
I. Chamberlain, Margaret, ill. II. Title. III. Series.
PZ7.Y8244Ri 1993
[E]—dc20
                                                93-5003
                                                CIP
                                                AC

Color reproduction by DOT Gradations Ltd.
Printed in Singapore

Mr. Richie F. Dweebly was a teacher. He wasn't very big or very handsome, but he was a nice young man and he loved teaching children.

Unfortunately, his students thought he was the most boring teacher on Earth.

As soon as he began to talk, the children couldn't stop yawning, the pet mouse snored, and even the class goldfish drifted to the bottom of his bowl and fell asleep.

Mr. Dweebly could make even the most interesting things, such as science experiments, dinosaurs, and ghost stories, so tedious that his class would begin to daydream and fidget.

As his voice droned on, they would pass photos of rock stars under their desks and whisper. Some children liked Rick Flick, others preferred Zoot Flash, and some thought Gary Vibes was super cool.

But they all agreed that the best was the great Rab Thunder. His music made you twitch your toes, wiggle your hips, and snap your fingers just thinking about it.

Mr. Dweebly never noticed his class passing photos and fan magazines. He never seemed to notice their buttons or the writing on their book bags and pencil cases that said FAB RAB THUNDERS ON. He would just go on in his monotonous way with nobody listening to him.

One day the children were supposed to be working on their weather project in groups – but nobody could remember what Mr. Dweebly had told them to do. Instead they talked some more about the fantabulous Rab Thunder.

"I bet he lives in a huge mansion with 50 rooms," said Sarah.

"And drives a Porsche!" said Amy.

"And a Rolls Royce on Sundays!"

Fab Rab

"I bet you he gets that amazing tan in the Caribbean."

"And he eats in fabulous restaurants, and orders just what he wants, and has loads of helpings if he wants to!"

"Yeah!" everyone agreed.

At the end of the lesson the class elected Sarah and Amy as President and Secretary of the school RAB THUNDER FAN CLUB because they had tickets for his concert that very evening.

Before the bell rang at the end of the day, Mr. Dweebly's dreary voice spoiled some good poetry and had the children nodding off while he told them about next week's visit to a fire station. At last they were free to go home and watch something interesting on TV or read an exciting book.

Mr. Dweebly bicycled home to his dull little house where he sat glumly eating baked beans on toast. He wondered why his students didn't seem to enjoy his lessons. After all, he spent so much of his time preparing for them.

But tonight was Friday night and he could think about things other than school.

He washed his one plate, one cup, one fork, one knife, and one spoon. Then he locked his front door and pedaled off on his bicycle, a big suitcase strapped on his back. It was nearly dark by the time he came to the local football stadium, where thousands of people were already streaming through the turnstiles. But Mr. Dweebly went around the back, chained his bike to a fence, and went in through the Players' Entrance.

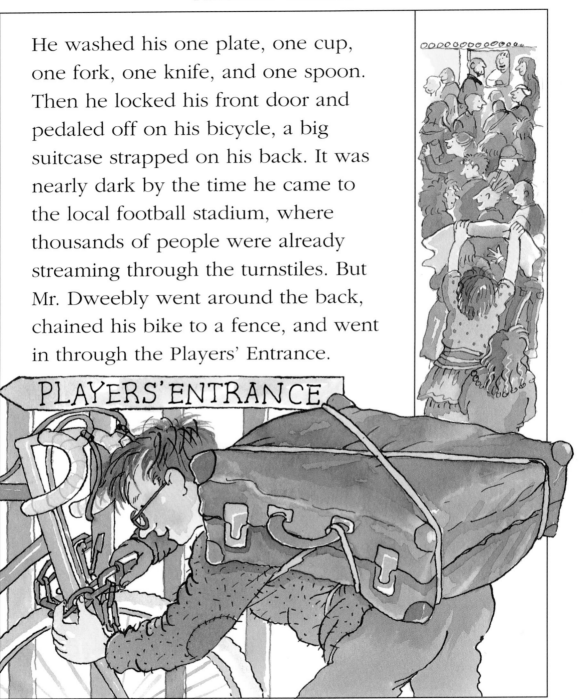

By nine o'clock, Richie F. Dweebly was sitting in front of a big mirror with light bulbs all around it. He was wearing just his underwear.

First he put on a hairy chest wig and a big gold chain. Next, he put on a purple shirt and skin-tight purple pants with glittery sequins sewn on. He pulled on shoes with platform soles and heels, and a purple jacket with gigantic shoulder pads and silver flashes all over it.

He still looked like Mr. Dweebly from the neck up. But not for long. He rubbed on some tan makeup from a pot marked "Caribbean Tan," put on his purple shades, and last of all, a wild black wig. When he stood up he looked enormous.

He took one last look at himself in the mirror.

Then he picked up an electric guitar and strode out the door.

The crowd screamed as the announcer yelled into his microphone . . .

AND NOW FANS, TOP OF THE BILL, THE ONE YOU'VE ALL BEEN WAITING FOR, THE ONE AND ONLY . . . THE ELECTRIFYING . . . RAB THUNDER AND THE THUNDERBOLTS!!!

The crowd went crazy!

Rab stamped his foot, the drummer took up the beat, the keyboards and back-up guitars joined in louder and louder until Rab began to roar out "Schoolroom Rock."

The crowd went berserk!

RAB!

Next Rab pounded into "Meet Me at the Bus Stop." He did a somersault while still playing the guitar. When he played "Lumpy Pudding Blues" he split his trousers, and at the end of "Listen When I'm Talkin' to Ya," fireworks exploded from his wig.

The fans sang along with every song. Of course, they knew them all by heart.

When Rab came to "Write Me a Letter," the crowd hushed. He moved to the front of the stage to be near his adoring fans. There, in the second row, sat Amy and Sarah, mouths open wide, soaking up every sound Rab made. He looked right at them and they swooned.

Then Rab strutted into his final song, "Homeroom." With a last crash on his guitar, a roll of drums, and a whirl of spotlights, the concert was over. The crowd went on cheering for half an hour.

Rab Thunder took off his shades, his black wig, and his tan makeup. Then he shed his big shoulders, purple shirt, and sequined pants. He took off the chest wig and gold chain, and stepped down off his platform shoes. Once again he was Richie F. Dweebly, sitting in his underwear.

He sat thinking for a long time.

On Monday morning the class came in chatting. Amy and Sarah had already told everyone about the concert.

Mr. Dweebly took attendance and the students prepared to be bored, as usual.

But then Mr. Dweebly picked up two rulers, did a drum roll on his desk and some paint jars, grabbed a guitar from behind his chair, plugged it in – and twanged out three loud chords!

Then he sang:

NOW LISTEN ALL YOU CHILDREN AND LISTEN REALLY GOOD! WHAT I'M GONNA TELL YOU MUST BE UNDERSTOOD!

The children, the white mouse, and even the goldfish sat up and took notice.

Mr. Dweebly sang on:

TODAY WE'RE LEARNING WITH A SWING. INSTEAD OF TALKING, I'M GONNA SING!

24

"The Romans had no volts at all,
Nothing plugged in a Roman wall.
No microwaves or color TVs,
No heaters, ovens, or loud CDs."

"If you were Roman, what'd you use
To cook your food or hear the news?
What'd you wear or have to drink?
Move to your groups and have a think."

The children couldn't believe their ears,
but they **did** go away and think.

In the afternoon, Mr. Dweebly began
the science lesson by singing:

"When we've planted a little black bean,
What does it need to make it grow?"

The children discussed it
and sang back:

A LOT OF LIGHT WILL MAKE IT GREEN
AND WATER,TOO—THAT'S H-2-O.

The students even enjoyed doing their multiplication tables when Mr. Dweebly told them:

"Clap your hands and stamp your feet,
Sing out your answers on the beat
To ten times five and three times two,
It's really easy, so try it, do!"

At three o'clock Mr. Dweebly sang:

"We've rocked and rolled together,
But now I hear the bell.
Pack up your things,
Stand by your chairs,
And I'll bid you all farewell."

And as the children filed out the door, they sang back:

IT'S BEEN A GREAT DAY'S WORK,

IT'S REALLY BEEN A TREAT.

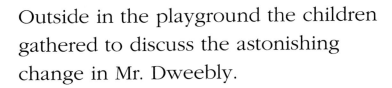

Outside in the playground the children gathered to discuss the astonishing change in Mr. Dweebly.

"Wow, that was amazing!"

"Where did he learn to sing and play guitar like that?"

"Yeah, he's almost as good as Rab Thunder," suggested one of the boys.

"Well, he's good, but he's not THAT good," said Amy loyally.

"Absolutely NOBODY is THAT good," said Sarah, "because Rab Thunder is the very best and don't you forget it!"

Mr. Dweebly, who was going
past on his bike, overheard
them—and smiled.